June 22, 2002

W9-CFH-326

Chandler

Bravo!

To our star of
the Ballet!
Congratulations
on your first
Recital . . .

XOXO
mommie &
Papa

Alice in Wonderland

The HARRIET TREASURY

A Collection of three classic books:

Harriet's Recital   Harriet & Walt

Harriet and the Roller Coaster

BARNES
&NOBLE
BOOKS
NEW YORK

HARRIET'S
· RECITAL ·

Nancy Carlson

for Susan Pearson, who has taught me
so-o-o much. Thanks!

This edition published by Barnes & Noble, Inc.
by arrangement with the Lerner Publishing Group

1998 Barnes & Noble Books

Harriet's Recital, Harriet & Walt, and *Harriet and the Roller Coaster*
all copyright © 1982 by CAROLRHODA BOOKS, INC.,
a division of the Lerner Publishing Group

Printed and bound in the United States of America
10   9   8   7   6   5   4   3   2   1

Harriet loved her ballet class . . .

. . . except for one thing. Once a year the class gave a recital. Harriet hated recitals.

"You'll do just fine, Harriet," said Miss Betty.
"No, I won't," said Harriet. "I'll trip."

All week long Harriet worried about the recital.

When she took a bath, she thought about falling.

When she saw her mother sewing her costume,

she worried that it would rip.

At last the big day arrived.

Harriet was terrified.

She knew she would never remember her dance.

The whole thing was a big mistake.

Everyone else in her class was ready.

Miss Betty was welcoming the audience.

"I can't do this," said Harriet

as the class danced onto the stage.

"Just take a deep breath and relax," said
Miss Betty.
"I can't," said Harriet.

"On you go," said Miss Betty.

"Oh, no," said Harriet.

"Take a deep breath," Miss Betty whispered
from offstage.

Harriet took one deep breath.

Then she took another.

She took one step ...

. . . then one more . . .

. . . and then . . .

. . . she was dancing!

"You were wonderful," said Harriet's father.
"Were you frightened?" said Harriet's mother.
"Not a bit," said Harriet, and they all went
out for a soda.

HARRIET &
· WALT ·

HARRIET &
· WALT ·

Nancy Carlson

for Gail, in memory of our winter in Norway

"Yippee!" yelled Harriet. "It must have snowed all night long! I'm going to play outside all day."

"Don't forget Walt," said Mother.
"Aw, Mom," said Harriet.

"Harriet," said her Mother. "You take your little brother with you, and that's final."

"Oh, all right," grumbled Harriet. "Come on, Walt."

"I'm going to make a tunnel through this snowdrift," said Harriet. "It's going to be so neat, Walt!"
And it was ...

. . . until Walt fell through it.
"You big dope," said Harriet.

Harriet decided to make a snow angel in-
stead. "Look, Walt. It's easy. You try it."

So Walt did.

"Not *that* way, Walt! Lie on your *back*," said Harriet. "Boy, oh boy, what a dummy."

"You said it!" said Harriet's friend George.
"Come on, Harriet. Let's play tag. But not
Walt. He's too little."

"Listen, Walt," said Harriet. "You stand right here by the flagpole and don't move. And whatever you do, don't put your tongue on the pole."

So Walt stood quietly by the flagpole. But pretty soon he got curious.

"Owwww!" screamed Walt.
"Boy," said George. "Walt is the dumbest little brother I've ever seen. Come on, Harriet. Let's build a snowman."

"Wowee!" said George. "This is going to be
the best snowman ever." And George might
have been right ...

... but Walt wrecked it.

"Walt, you are so stupid," said George.
"He was only trying to help," said Harriet.

"Come on," said George. "Let's go sliding.
Walt can't wreck that."

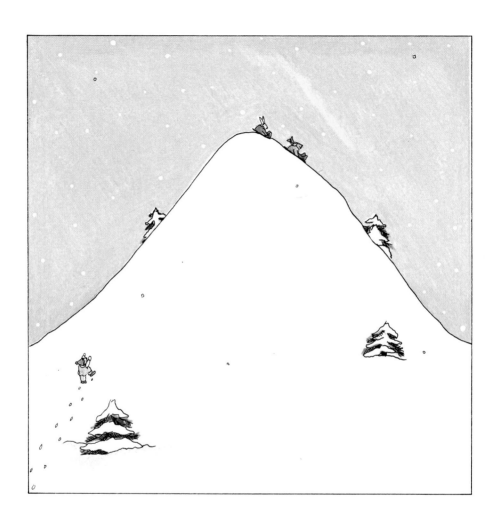

So they all climbed the hill. It took Walt a long time.

Harriet and George were already at the
bottom again when Walt started down.
"Oh, no," said Harriet. "I can't look."

"Boy, what a jerk," said George. "Can't he do anything right?"

"George," said Harriet. "He can't help it. He's just little, that's all."
"He's just dumb," said George.

"Come on, Walt," said Harriet. "Let's go home."

On the way, Harriet taught Walt how to make a snow angel.

And she helped him build a snowman.

And she took him down a hill on her card-
board.

When they got home, it was almost supper time.

"Well," said Mother. "Did you have a good time?"

"Once we got rid of that dumb George we did," said Harriet. "Didn't we, Walt?"

But Walt was fast asleep.

HARRIET and the ROLLER COASTER

HARRIET and the
ROLLER COASTER

Nancy Carlson

for Jeanne and Mary,
because they take the chances I don't!

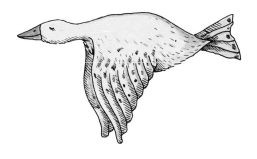

On the last day of school, Harriet's whole
class was going to the amusement park.
Everyone looked forward to the day.

"I'm going to ride on the big roller coaster," George told Harriet. "It's so big, you can't see the top. I know. My big sister told me."

"It goes so fast that if you don't hold on you'll fall right out."

"I bet you're too scared to ride the roller coaster. You'd probably start crying."

"I am *not* scared," said Harriet. "I'll ride on your old roller coaster. You just wait and see."

That night Harriet didn't sleep very well.

The next morning, when it was time to get on the bus for the amusement park, she felt a little sick.

"See you on the roller coaster," said George. "If you don't chicken out."

As soon as they got to the amusement park, George said, "Come on, Harriet. Let's get our tickets for the roller coaster. Unless you're too scared."

"I am *not* scared," said Harriet.

"Good," said George. "Then hurry up."

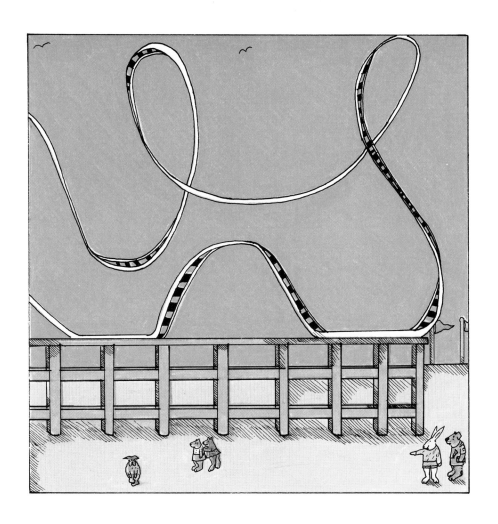

"Oh, boy," said George.

"I can't wait!"

"We're next. . . .

There's still time for you to chicken out."

"Here we go. Harriet, you're going to be sooooo scared."

The roller coaster went up and up. Harriet
had never been so high.

"This is great," said George.

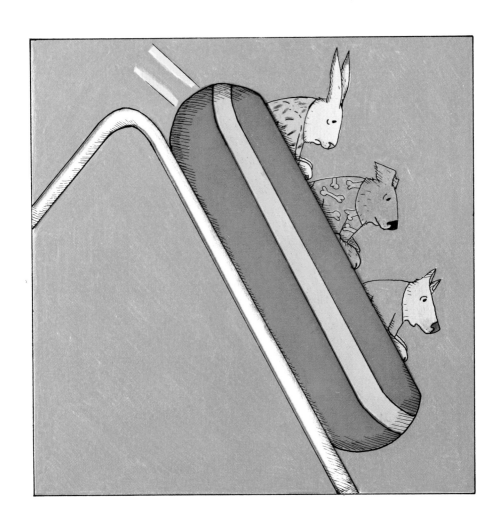

Then they were over the top.

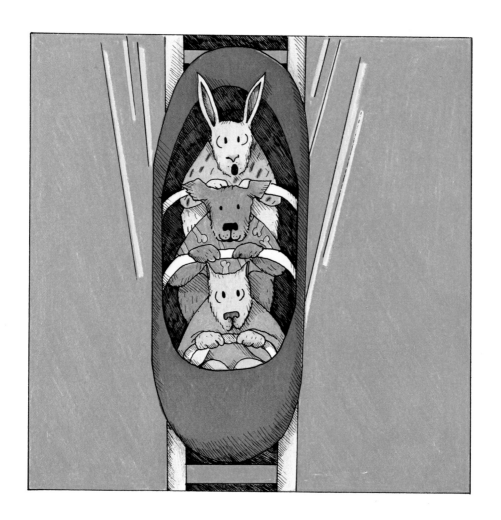

"Hey!" said Harriet. "This isn't so bad."
"Ooof!" said George.

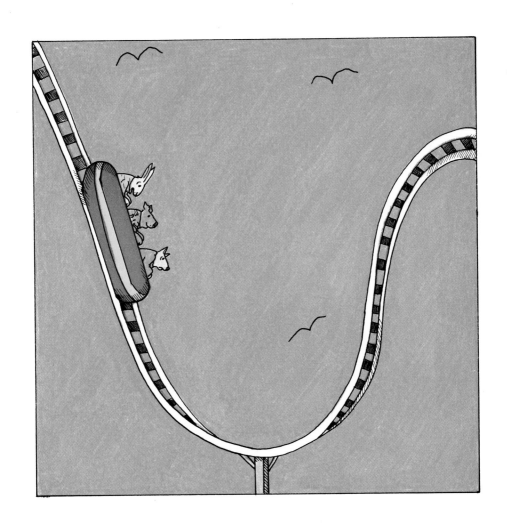

"I like it!" said Harriet.
"Help!" said George.

"Yippee!" yelled Harriet.
"Mommy!" yelled George.

"Is it over already?" said Harriet.

"I'm going again. That was fun!"
"I'd better sit down," said George.

So Harriet rode the roller coaster all day
long . . .

... while George sat quietly on a bench.